WEST SIDE ZOMBIE

"These violent delights have violent ends"

Romeo and Juliet, Act 2 Scene 6

Titles in Dark Reads:

Blood Moon
Barbara Catchpole

The Black-Eyed Girl
Tim Collins

Something Rotten
Tim Collins

Storm Bringer
Tim Collins

West Side Zombie
Tim Collins

Ringtone
Tommy Donbavand

The Girl in the Wall
Tommy Donbavand

MC Cesar
Tommy Donbavand

Red Handed
Ann Evans

Straw Men
Ann Evans

Kicked Into Touch
Ann Evans

**Doctor Jekyll and
Little Miss Hyde**
Tony Lee

Otis
Tony Lee

Bright Lights
Claire Morgan

Titan
Danny Pearson

Ship of the Dead
Alex Woolf

Badger Publishing Limited, Oldmedow Road, Hardwick Industrial Estate, King's Lynn PE30 4JJ
Telephone: 01438 791037

www.badgerlearning.co.uk

West Side Zombie ISBN 978-1-78464-433-8

Text © Tim Collins 2016
Complete work © Badger Publishing Limited 2016

Publisher: Susan Ross
Senior Editor: Danny Pearson
Editorial Coordinator: Claire Morgan
Copyeditor: Cheryl Lanyon
Designer: Bigtop Design Ltd
Illustrator: Aleksandar Sotirovski

2 4 6 8 10 9 7 5 3

WEST SIDE ZOMBIE

TIM COLLINS

Illustrated by Aleksandar Sotirovski

Contents

CHAPTER 1
BITTEN

Romeo and Juliet sprinted away from the zombies.

Juliet looked back. There were five of the creatures. They had escaped from the compound in the west of town and were racing towards them with their rotting grey hands stretched out.

Juliet fell to the ground.

A cold hand grabbed the back of her neck. Jagged fingernails pressed into her skin.

Juliet twisted round to see the creature's black gums and sharp yellow teeth.

She had to get away. If she was bitten, she would become infected and turn into a zombie herself.

A gunshot rang out and the creature's head burst like a rotten melon.

The army was here.

Juliet got up and wiped her face. Romeo was a few feet ahead. There was a fresh bite mark on his arm.

CHAPTER 2
INFECTED

Juliet pressed Romeo's wound. The skin around it was grey and felt freezing cold.

They were standing on the balcony of her bedroom.

"This isn't safe for you," said Romeo. "I have to go to the compound."

"It could be weeks before you change," said Juliet. "Don't go yet."

Juliet's father stepped out of the front door. He heard his daughter and her boyfriend talking on the balcony above.

Anger welled inside him. He couldn't believe she'd let one of those creatures into his house.

He had to do something.

CHAPTER 3
BETRAYED

Juliet woke with a start. She had dozed off. Romeo was gone.

Juliet went to her balcony.

"Where are you?" she muttered.

The door to her bedroom swung open and her father stomped in.

"Your zombie boyfriend isn't coming back," he said. "I told him you never want to see him again and he's gone to the compound."

Juliet sank down on her bed and pushed her face into her pillow. Tears ran down her cheeks.

She'd never see Romeo again. If he tried to leave the compound, the guards would shoot him.

She wished she'd been bitten too. Then at least they'd still be together.

This gave her an idea.

CHAPTER 4
DISGUISED

Juliet shuffled towards the compound.

She'd spent all day painting her skin grey, drawing cracked veins on her cheeks and dabbing fake blood around her mouth.

She was sure the guards would think she was a zombie. They'd let her in and she'd be able to see Romeo one last time.

Juliet turned the corner. The entrance to the compound was straight ahead.

A guard stepped into her path and raised his gun.

"Escaped zombie ahead," he shouted into the microphone in his helmet. "I'm going to take it out."

"Don't shoot!" shouted Juliet. "It's just a disguise."

She ran her fingers down her cheek, smudging grey makeup onto her fingers.

"Look," she said.

She held her hand out and stepped towards the guard.

He pulled the trigger.

CHAPTER 5
REUNITED

Romeo heard the gunshot and looked out of the compound gate.

In the street beyond, he saw Juliet fall backwards. A patch of deep red was spreading across her chest.

He rushed out.

"Stop!" shouted the guard. "Get back inside."

Juliet's body had gone still by the time Romeo reached her.

He ran his fingers down her face and grey paint rubbed off. He realised she'd disguised herself as a zombie to come and see him.

Her father had lied.

He leaned forwards to kiss her cheek.

"Stand up and put your hands above your head or we'll shoot," shouted the guard.

Romeo cradled Juliet's body. A tear ran down his nose and splashed onto her face. He no longer cared if he died.

The guard aimed his gun at Romeo's head and fired.

STORY FACTS

This story was inspired by William Shakespeare's famous play *Romeo and Juliet*, which was published in 1597.

It was also inspired by zombie films such as *Night of the Living Dead*, which was directed by George A. Romero in 1968.

Until *Night of the Living Dead*, zombies had been shown as slaves under the power of a witch doctor. The film set up the idea of them as flesh-eating creatures that came back from the dead.

Romeo and Juliet also inspired *West Side Story*, a 1959 musical by Leonard Bernstein and Stephen Sondheim. It featured classic songs such as 'America' and 'Maria'.

QUESTIONS

What are Romeo and Juliet running
away from?
(page 7)

What colour are the zombie's gums?
(page 8)

Why does Romeo leave for the compound?
(page 14)

How does Juliet make herself look like
a zombie?
(page 18)

Where does the guard shoot Romeo?
(page 28)

MEET THE AUTHOR

Tim Collins has written over 50 books for children and adults, including *Wimpy Vampire*, *Cosmic Colin*, *Monstrous Maud* and *Dorkius Maximus*. His other teenage fiction for Badger Learning includes The *Black-Eyed Girl*, *Joke Shop* and *Mr Perfect*. Tim has won awards in the UK and Germany.

MEET THE ARTIST

Aleksandar Sotirovski is from Macedonia. He is an illustrator with over 25 years' experience. He has worked on lots of children's books, textbooks and posters. He is also a concept artist for comics and games.